MW01142176

BUSTER BOPPINGTON
and his TALKING DOG
in the Case of the
IMPOSSIBLE BANK ROBBERY

BY BRUCE CAPLAN

SEATTLE MIRACLE PRESS

Published by
  Seattle Miracle Press, Inc.
  4976 120th Avenue S.E.
  Bellevue, Washington 98006

Buster Boppington and his Talking Dog is a work of fiction.
All characters and events are imaginary. Any resemblance to
persons living or dead is coincidental.

Copyright ©1995 by Seattle Miracle Press, Inc.
All rights reserved.

ISBN: 0-9644610-0-5

Special Thanks To:
  Elaine Mahler
  Karen McGinn
  Everett Greiman
  Kimberlee Colin

Production by Dataprose Typesetting, Seattle, Washington

To my family
Esther
Brianna and Rachel
Maybelle and Al
&
Napoleon (Nappy)

CHAPTER 1
THE BANK ROBBERY

It was an upsetting day for 9-year-old Buster Boppington. To begin with, his radio-alarm clock did not awaken him on time and, even though he rode his 24-inch red bicycle as fast as his feet could spin the pedals, he arrived at school 15 minutes late. Because of his tardiness, he had to go to the principal's office and tell Miss Madill, the skinny gray-haired secretary, why he was late. He stared at the ugly woman for a moment. To Buster, Miss Madill looked like a combination of George Washington and a witch.

"Buster Boppington, this is the fourth time this month you have been late to school. If this tardiness continues, I shall be forced to schedule a conference between your parents and the principal," Miss Madill said.

Buster swallowed a few times. He could feel his heart racing. "Miss Madill, please don't call my parents. Dad's been out of work for ages, and the reason I'm late so much is that my clock radio's broken."

The old lady gazed at the boy. Her voice was soothing. "Buster, you may go to your class now. Don't worry. You're excused this time. Just don't fret about your father's troubles. Everything always seems to work out for the best."

As Buster entered the classroom, he sensed all the children's eyes on him. He knew that many of them were happy that he had to report to the office. Buster decided to look sad so the mean kids would think he had been punished for breaking the rules.

It wasn't difficult for Buster to appear unhappy. Last year in the third grade, he was one of the best students in the class, but this year his grades had fallen to near the bottom. He knew the reason his studies had slipped so badly.

His problems began about two months before. It had been a sunny August Monday, and Buster and his friend Jamie were going fishing for trout in Lake Washington. The boys had taken branches from a large maple tree in Buster's back yard and tied fishing line and leader to them to make fishing poles. Everything was ready for their great adventure when Buster heard the roar of his father's old Buick as it entered their driveway. Something must be wrong, Buster thought—his father never came home at 11 in the morning.

Buster watched as his father slowly opened the door of the car and stepped out. A minute later, he saw his pretty blonde mother run to join her husband. Buster ran up to them, too.

Within moments he learned that his father had been fired from the bank where he had worked for most of Buster's life. His dad had worked his way up to the position of head teller, which put him in charge of all the money in the bank. That Monday morning, Mr. Boppington told them, he had entered the large vault where the money was stored. To his shock, almost all the currency was gone from the place where he had locked it up the previous Friday night.

On and off all the rest of that day, Buster listened to his father tell the story of what had happened after the discovery of the theft. He felt as if he had been there with his dad and the bank president as Buster's father received the terrible news.

Buster sat in the big leather rocking chair and his parents sat on the couch. His father nervously ran his fingers through his thick dark hair and said, "After the discovery of the missing funds, I was called into Mr. Gonifman's office. He was furious and glared at me. The bum never smiles. 'Sidney . . . Sidney Boppington, how long have you been with our bank?' he growled.

"I swallowed and told him that this was the only real job that I've ever had. I reminded him that I'd been working there almost eight years. Then I said, 'Remember, sir, I started working here just after graduating from the University.'

"Gonifman was silent for a moment, and then said, 'Last Friday you were the only one in the bank after closing hours. You shut the vault and you, Sid Boppington, verified that all the money was in the vault when you locked it. Since the vault is on a time-lock for 60 hours after the door is closed, it's impossible for anyone to rob the bank after the vault is shut. This morning when you and I and the rest of the employees entered the vault most of the money was gone. Boppington, we don't believe in magic at this bank, and logic tells me that you've stolen over $100,000. I've contacted the local and federal authorities. You are hereby terminated from your position. Stealing funds is a federal offense and you'll probably have to spend time in prison for what you've done.' As Mr. Gonifman finished speaking he made a motion with both of his arms for me to leave the bank immediately."

After the bank robbery Mr. Boppington tried to find work. Each morning he would put on his finest suit and look at the newspaper in hopes of finding the best available positions. At the end of the second month, he was very discouraged. It seemed that all the people offering jobs had phoned Mr. Gonifman. Gonifman had told them that Mr. Boppington was a man who could not be trusted and that very soon he would probably be in jail.

One afternoon after school, when Buster turned his large brass key in the lock on the front door and went inside, he heard sobs coming from the kitchen. He ran to his weeping mother and tried to comfort her. "Mom," he said, "I know why you're upset. Daddy's out of work. Don't worry. He can find a good job."

Buster's mother held on to him tightly. "Sweetheart, I wasn't crying because your father hasn't found a job. In my heart, I know he'll find something, if only the authorities will let him. About 10 minutes ago the FBI telephoned. They want your father to take a lie-detector test tomorrow morning. He doesn't have to take the test if he doesn't want to, but if he doesn't take it everyone will think he's guilty."

Later, when Mr. Boppington came home and his wife told him about the call from the FBI, Buster watched his father's complexion change from its normal olive to a deep red. Then he coughed and cleared his throat. "I'll take the polygraph test. I checked with my friend Bill Brawer who works at the police station. He told me that lie-detector tests are not always accurate. If I fail it they can't use that as evidence in court, but if I pass it, there's a good chance the police and FBI will drop their investigation against me."

"Oh, Sidney," exclaimed Mrs. Boppington, "that means that if you pass the test tomorrow, you'll get your job back?"

Buster looked into his father's eyes hoping to see him smile. Instead there was sadness. "Even if I pass the test, that won't convince Gonifman I'm innocent, and that means he'll continue to bad-mouth me when I try to find a job. It's lucky for us that we still have some savings left. If we budget ourselves, we can survive a couple of months without too much difficulty."

That night as Buster lay in bed, he was very nervous. He wanted so much to help his mother and father, but he couldn't think of any way to be of assistance.

CHAPTER 2
THE LIE-DETECTOR TEST

I t was 6 a.m. when Buster awoke to the sound of shuffling feet in his bedroom. He knew the test his father was to take today was more important than any Buster had ever taken in school.

Soon his mother stood by his bed with a big smile on her face. "Sweetheart, today things may really improve in this family. You'll have to get ready for school on your own. I left you a bowl of cereal in the kitchen. Just add a cup of milk to it and put your dish in the sink when you're done. And remember to put the milk back in the fridge."

Buster coughed a couple of times. Then he swallowed a few times. He didn't feel up to going to school today. He was too nervous. He stretched the truth and told his mother that he had a very bad sore throat.

She seemed to understand. "Buster, you've been wonderful during our family crisis, and I think it'll be all right if you stay home and rest for a day. I'll give you some warm chocolate milk, and later you can go into the den and watch television." Buster noticed a tiny teardrop slide down her cheek.

Buster was restless as he waited for his parents' return from the lie-detector test. After almost four hours of trying to keep himself distracted, he heard the front door open and he rushed to greet his parents. "Daddy," he yelled, "did you pass? Do they know that you didn't steal the money at the bank?"

Buster's eager eyes were met by a disappointed expression. "I thought I'd find out the results of the test today," his father told him. "Unfortunately, the FBI agent told us that it'll take at least a couple of days."

The following two days were terribly tense in the Boppington house. Buster sensed that his parents were about to explode. He did the best he could to keep his room clean and stay out of the way. The phone must have rang 20 times on the second afternoon. Each time, Mrs. Boppington raced to the phone and prayed that the FBI would be on the other end of the line. About 4:30 in the afternoon her prayers were finally answered.

Buster watched his mother intently as she listened. When she hung up the phone, tears were pouring down her face. Suddenly she blurted, "He's clear! He's clear! The lie-detector test has proven Daddy did not steal the money. He probably will not have to go to jail!"

CHAPTER 3
THE BIRTHDAY PRESENTS

September 23 was Buster's 10th birthday. On all his other birthdays he remembered big parties with lots of presents and many friends to celebrate with. Because of his father's troubles he was fairly certain that his 10th birthday was going to be a very sad affair.

That morning when Buster awoke he realized with some pride that he would no longer be able to put his age on paper using just one digit. In six years he would be old enough to drive a car. His thoughts were interrupted as the door of his room was pushed open. His parents walked to the foot of his bed and sang "Happy Birthday."

Buster kept hearing a funny squeaking sound. It was such a strange noise that for a moment it scared him until he saw where it was coming from. A little brown-haired poodle raced into his room and jumped on his bed. Buster smiled, and for the first time in many, many weeks, the Boppington family felt that life was getting better.

He named his dog Napoleon because the animal was so small and short, but like the great French emperor of the same name the dog appeared to be strong and intelligent. "Nappy, come here," he gushed, and the little dog's bobbed tail wagged excitedly as he scampered over to Buster.

At school that day Buster's classes seemed easier. When the 3:10 bell rang, he raced home to see Nappy. When he ran up the front yard he found a brown paper package next to the screen door and was surprised to see that it was addressed to him. It was from his uncle, a scientist for a chemical company, who lived in Brooklyn, New York. Buster had only met him once, and that was when he was 4 years old. He could hardly remember what his uncle looked like.

When he went in the house Nappy bounded up to him and stretched his paws up on Buster's legs so Buster could grab them. Nappy had only been in the house a few hours, but already he was Buster's best friend. He petted Nappy for a while and then gently pushed him aside. With the package under his arm, he ran to the kitchen where the aroma of freshly baked bread filled his nostrils. His mother turned away from the stove and smiled at him. "Well, I see that you and Napoleon are going to be lifelong friends." She bent down and kissed Buster's cheek. "Where did that package come from?"

"Mom, it's from Uncle Morrie in New York. Usually he sends me $10 for my birthday, but this year he sent me a real present. May I open it now? Getting Nappy and now a box from New York . . . you know, Mommy, this is one of the best birthdays that I can remember!"

"Dear, Daddy's been out all day looking for a job. Watching you open a gift may be just the prescription to make him feel better. Do you mind waiting until tonight to unwrap the package?"

Buster laughed. "Gee you're right, Mom. I'll open it later."

That evening Buster opened the package as his parents watched. He eagerly cut the string and removed the brown paper wrapping. His eyes gazed upon a shiny blue metal case. Buster was disappointed. He thought his uncle had mailed him a tool kit for doing repairs around the house. But when he opened the case, he saw, to his amazement, about 35 bottles with all sorts of different colored powders in them. "What's this?" he wondered.

His father scratched his head. "Son, I think Uncle Morrie has sent you a chemistry set."

Mrs. Boppington was concerned. "Chemistry sets can be very dangerous," she said.

"How?" Buster asked.

Mr. Boppington explained. "Everything in the world is made of chemicals. The problem is that if the powders are mixed in the wrong way they could poison someone or even blow them up. Son, you're 10 years old today, but I want you to wait until you're at least 14 to use this gift. A chemistry set can be very educational, but those powders are for experiments and experiments can be dangerous unless you know what you're doing."

Buster looked at the floor, thinking to himself, "It's my birthday, and I got a gift that I can't use for another four years."

"Maybe he can do a couple of small experiments next week," his mother suggested, and Buster could see she understood his curiosity about the present.

"Dear, if you watch him closely Buster may try a couple of experiments," Mr. Boppington said.

About a week later Buster came home from school but could not find his mother. "Mom! Mommy! Where are you?" he yelled. But after a thorough search he realized that he and

Nappy were the only ones home.

Buster did not have any homework so he turned on the TV. He switched from channel to channel, but could find only boring programs. He went to his bedroom to take a nap.

About five minutes passed and Buster realized he really wasn't sleepy, he was just bored. Nappy came into his room and tried to jump on the bed, but Buster shooed him away. Not knowing what else to do he got up and headed for the living room. As he passed the coat closet, something caught his eye. There on the floor of the closet was the gleaming metal box that held the mysteries of his chemistry set. For several moments he just stared at the enchanting box. Then, slowly, his fingers began to move toward the shiny case.

On the one hand he told himself he should leave the chemistry set alone, but on the other hand, he thought, there was no harm in just looking at the bottles.

Buster took the set to his room and began to read the manual. He took out several bottles and placed them on his bedspread. When he got to page 14 he spotted an experiment that looked interesting. By mixing tannic acid and another chemical, he read, he could make ink. What harm, he figured, could possibly come from just mixing up a small batch of ink?

Buster looked all over the house for some bowls to mix the chemicals in, but he couldn't find a glass or dish that he thought his mother would allow him to use for experiments. He was in the kitchen when he saw it: There next to the garage door was a yellow bowl that was half filled with water.

Buster looked at Nappy and the happy dog returned his gaze with big brown eyes. "Hey pal," Buster said, "may I use your water bowl for awhile. Nappy wagged his tail, which Buster figured meant yes in dog language.

For more than half an hour Buster feverishly tried to make ink. Regardless of how carefully he followed the directions, the liquid in the bowl continued to look like plain water. Suddenly, Buster heard the sound of his mother's key in the door. He quickly shoved the bottles of chemicals back into their case and slammed the box shut. Fortunately for Buster, his mother, upon entering the house, ran straight to the bathroom. This gave him enough time to race to the hall closet and put the chemistry set back where he found it.

Later that day a very sad Mr. Boppington came home. He told his wife and son that he had almost gotten a good job, but when his new employer phoned Mr. Gonifman for a reference, he told the man that Mr. Boppington was a thief. Because of Gonifman's bad recommendation, the job offer was withdrawn.

CHAPTER 4
NAPPY TALKS

The three Boppingtons barely touched their meals that evening. Nappy sensed something was wrong but that didn't stop the little dog from gobbling up all his food. After Nappy finished his meal, he was thirsty. As he drank the water in his bowl, it tasted funny to him. Suddenly he realized why: Buster had forgotten to remove his experiment from the dish. Nappy became frightened; he might be poisoned by Buster's experiment. He wanted desperately to tell Buster what had happened so something could be done to make sure he would not die. Unfortunately, Nappy could not talk. Shaking from fear, the little animal went to his soft bed in the basement to rest, and, oh yes, to pray.

It was about 3 o'clock in the morning when Nappy awoke. He had been having terrible dreams. In one he died and went to animal heaven. In another nightmare he pictured himself drinking poison. As he lay awake he thought how stupid Buster had been for putting harmful chemicals in his water. Nappy wanted to live a long, wonderful life. He feared that what Buster had done would kill him.

That thought made him overcome by anger. Without thinking about what he was doing, he raced upstairs and into Buster's room. He scratched at the sleeping boy to wake him up. Buster rolled over and began to mumble softly in his sleep. Nappy gave his master a hard shove with his paws. Buster remained asleep. In frustration, the dog yelled, "Buster, wake up, you fool, wake up."

The sound of Nappy's voice had the desired effect. Buster turned toward his dog. His eyes were now open but his mind was foggy. "What is it, Nappy? What's wrong?"

"I'll tell you what's wrong! You poisoned my water and on account of what you've done I might die!"

"Nappy, try to keep your voice down. You might wake Dad, and he has another interview tomorrow."

"I'm sorry, Buster, it's just that I was so frightened of dying, because you left your experiment in my bowl."

It finally dawned on Buster what was happening. "You're talking! You're talking! That's crazy, dogs can't talk!" he squealed.

A voice came from Buster's parents' bedroom. "Buster, are you having a nightmare?" his father yelled.

"No, Dad, I just had a crazy dream. I dreamed that Nappy could talk."

Mr. Boppington laughed and said, "Pleasant dreams."

"Pleasant dreams, Dad," Buster replied as he put his head back on his pillow. He looked at the clock and saw he only had about three hours to sleep before he had to get up for school. As he lay in bed, he thought about the peculiar dream he had just had. He wondered what ever could cause him to dream that Nappy could speak.

He had just about dropped off to sleep again when he heard someone whispering. This strange voice said, "Miracle of miracles, I can talk. I really can talk."

Buster bolted upright. Soon his eyes focused on Nappy. The dog was looking up at him and speaking. "Buster those powders you mixed in your experiment have given me the ability to talk. At first I was really angry at you for letting me drink the dangerous water. I'm less angry now because I'm sure that I am the world's first talking dog."

Buster just stared at Nappy for a moment. "I'm sorry that I forgot to change your water. It was just that Mom surprised me and after I threw the chemistry set back, I forgot that I had mixed my experiment in your bowl. . . . Nappy, we can't let anyone know you can talk. If Mommy or Daddy finds out, I'll be in gobs of trouble because I wasn't supposed to use the chemistry set."

"Buster you're right. I love you and you're my master. I'll never do anything to hurt you. I think we should sleep now. I have a feeling my new ability is going to be very helpful."

It was 6:30 in the morning and for once Buster's radio-alarm clock was working properly. The boy tossed and turned for a moment, then jumped out of the covers as he remembered what had happened just a few hours before. He looked under his bed and saw Nappy sound asleep. He reached his hand out to awaken his pet but quickly pulled his fingers away. He suddenly had doubts that Nappy could really speak. He told himself it was probably just a dream, remembering that he once had a dream that he had been given a brand new English-racer bicycle. The dream had been so real. But when he awoke, to his sadness, there was no bike. There was only his bedroom and a clock that told him he had to be to school in 30 minutes.

Fearful of another disappointment like that, he slowly reached his fingers out to pet his dog. He gently massaged Nappy's neck and then heard words that made his heart leap for joy. "That feels wonderful," Nappy said happily, and Buster Boppington knew for sure that he was the owner of the world's first talking dog.

A few minutes later, at breakfast with his mother and father, he tried to eat his oatmeal but he was just too excited to swallow. Nappy sat under the table and Buster sneaked him a buttered piece of toast. Nappy was just about to say "Thank you" when he realized he had promised he would speak only to Buster.

Mr. Boppington broke the silence. "I have that big interview with Boeing today. I think I have a good chance at getting the job."

"Dear, do you have any contacts at Boeing?" Mrs. Boppington asked.

"As a matter of fact, I do have some influence there," Mr. Boppington replied. "When I worked at the bank I took care of a lot of the company's accounts and many of their executives often told Mr. Gonifman what a good job I was doing. My interview tomorrow is with one of the men I used to serve. There just may be a chance that I can get the position." Buster noticed an element of desperation in his father's voice.

CHAPTER 5
NAPPY, BUSTER'S BEST FRIEND

That evening at dinner, Mr. Boppington was so happy he looked as if he could fly. Over and over he repeated details of his interview at Boeing. Nappy was under the table hoping for some scraps of food to fall on the floor. The young dog could understand Mr. Boppington's enthusiasm and was thrilled for his family.

Later that evening, when Buster had finished his homework and he and Nappy were quietly talking, Buster said, "Nappy, in just a few days most of the kids in my class are taking a trip to Snoqualmie Falls. That place is awesome."

"Buster, I don't understand. The way you talk . . . well it's like you're not going to go on this wonderful trip."

"Nappy, the trip isn't cheap. I can't afford to go." Buster laughed. "I don't know if you've noticed, but things have been a wee bit tight around here in the money department. Maybe you can tell me how to earn the $37 to go on the trip."

• Buster watched as Nappy's big brown eyes took on a look that was wiser than any of Buster's teachers. Suddenly the young dog exclaimed, "The horses, the horses! Of course, the horses at the racetrack. You need money and the track pays people who pick the winning horses at the races."

"Nappy, that's great, all you have to do is tell me who is going to win at the races and then I'll have all the money in the world," Buster giggled.

"Don't make fun of me," Nappy snapped. "I don't always know who's going to win at the track, but when I do know the winner, it's a sure thing."

"Nappy," Buster said, still chuckling, "you have my permission to tell me all the winners you know of."

"I have a friend who works at the track," Nappy said excitedly. "Tomorrow I'll go there and see what I can find out. In the meantime, my friend, you and I need sleep."

The next morning at breakfast, Mrs. Boppington said, "Buster, when I passed your room last night I heard a strange voice. Are you learning a new voice for a play at school or something?"

Buster choked on his cereal and some went flying out of his mouth and onto the floor. When he had composed himself, he sputtered, "Mom, I'm studying to be a ventriloquist. I saw this man on the television. He had a dummy, and I thought they were so funny that I decided to learn how to do it."

For a moment Mrs. Boppington studied her son. Buster saw the amazement in her eyes. "I'll never understand the miracles of this Earth. I thought you were just a regular, everyday child, and here you are studying a talent that the world will love to hear." Mrs. Boppington turned to her husband.

"Sid, listen to what our young man can do. Buster, speak in the voice you used last night."

Buster's face turned red. He was trapped. There was no way he could imitate Nappy's voice. He looked down at his dog and watched as the poodle's eyes looked first at him and then suggestively at the clock. "Gee, Mom," Buster found himself saying, "I'd love to talk with the other voice, but if I do I'll be late to school. How about later?"

"You're right, dear," his mother said, though she was a little disappointed. "You can show us when you come home from school."

Soon after Buster left, Nappy scratched at the front door and Mrs. Boppington let him out. It was a cold cloudy morning as the young dog briskly headed for the racetrack. It took him more than two hours to get there. It was about 11:30 when he spotted his friend Fritz Hellman. Fritz was a beautiful collie who helped out at the track. Nappy trotted up to Fritz and said nonchalantly, "How's my pal?"

For a moment Fritz did not recognize Nappy, but then he smiled. "Well, as I live and breathe, if it isn't Prince Thompson. Golly, it sure is great to see you. How are things over at the Thompson house?"

"Gee, Fritz," Nappy said, "I live with the Boppington family now and they've named me Napoleon."

Fritz smiled again. "You mean you're no longer living with Detective Thompson of the Seattle Police Department?"

"That's right." Nappy said. "Detective Thompson retired a few months ago and now I have a wonderful new home, though things have been kind of rough for the people in the house. Mr. Boppington got a bum rap at the bank and lost his job. Buster, his son, needs money to go on a class trip to Snoqualmie Falls."

Fritz looked concerned. "I guess you're looking for a sure winner. It's been a long time since you asked me for help."

"Fritz," Nappy said, "I figured if anyone would be on good terms with the horses it would be you."

"You know," Fritz said, "in the fifth race tomorrow, a horse named Puddinhead Putterman is running. He hasn't won a race in three years and all the horses feel sorry for him. If he loses tomorrow he'll be dog food by next week. He's going to win and I know that the odds on him will be more than 100 to one. Bet on him!"

By the time Nappy got back from the track, Buster was home from school and he immediately told Buster the good news.

"That's wonderful," Buster said. "I could be rich by to-morrow, except for a couple of things. Number one, I don't have any money to bet on the horses and, number two, even if I did have some dough, I'm not old enough to go to the track and bet on a horse."

"Buster, there's an old saying, 'Where there's a will there's a way,' " Nappy winked.

CHAPTER 6
THE BET

It was dinnertime. Nappy and Buster had laid out a thorough plan on how to get Mr. Boppington interested in betting at the track. Mr. Boppington was chewing away at a juicy lamb chop when his meal was interrupted by Buster. "Daddy, what does it mean when people tell you that they have ESP?"

Mr. Boppington put his lamb chop down on the side of his plate and looked at his son. "Buster, ESP stands for 'extra sensory perception.' Scientists think that thousands of years ago almost everybody had the power to communicate their thoughts without talking. Myself, I don't believe that there is any such a phenomenon."

"Dear," Mrs. Boppington said, "I don't see why you have to use such big words with Buster. Furthermore, I believe in ESP. Remember when we first met at the beach? I knew then and there that you and I were going to get married."

Mr. Boppington laughed and said, "Come to think of it, at that time, I had some ESP myself."

"Daddy", Buster said, "I have these funny dreams all the time. I keep dreaming that I'm at a place where horses race and my horse starts the race way in the back and then when the race is finished my horse always wins."

Mr. Boppington gave a hearty laugh. "My gosh, son, when I was your age I used to dream of winning football and baseball games. Times sure have changed."

"Daddy," Buster said, undeterred, "last night I had the strangest dream ever. I bet at the racetrack and my horse came in first. I dreamed that I had the winning ticket at the racetrack and I won more than $200."

"That's pretty amazing," Mrs. Boppington said. "If you knew the name of the horse in your dream, I'd be willing to take you to the racetrack and place a bet for you."

"That's just it," Buster blurted. "I think I can remember the name of the horse, it's . . ." Buster pretended to be concentrating. "It's . . . Puddinhead Putterman, the winner in the fifth race tomorrow." Buster prayed silently for his mother to keep her promise and take him to the track.

A short while later, Mr. Boppington was thumbing through the evening paper. When he got to the sports pages, he called out excitedly, "My gosh, there's a horse called Puddinhead Putterman in the fifth race tomorrow. Buster, I still doubt it, but maybe there's something to this ESP."

The following afternoon, Mr. and Mrs. Boppington eagerly waited for Buster outside his school. When the 3:10 bell rang, the three Boppingtons headed for the racetrack. As they entered the gate Buster was amazed at all the people at the races. He marveled at how well-kept and large the track was. Buster felt that everything was so wonderful, except that

Nappy, his miracle dog Nappy, was not with them.

The Boppingtons arrived in time for the first race. Watching the beautiful horses gallop around the track made Buster even more excited. An announcer told everybody which horse was leading at different times of the race. Buster was amazed at how quickly the race was over.

Some people applauded, but most of the crowd seemed to be disinterested in the result or upset by their loses.

It took almost an hour and a half before the fifth race was ready to begin. Mrs. Boppington leaned over and asked her husband, "What does it mean when the tote board says our horse has 99-to-1 odds?"

Before Mr. Boppington could answer, Buster interrupted, "That means if we win the race, they'll pay us at least $100 for each dollar we bet."

"Buster," Mrs. Boppington chuckled, "how did you get to know so much about the races? Have you been hanging around with some wild boys and girls?" She chuckled again. "Does that mean that we'll win more than $200.00 if our horse comes in first?"

"That's right, Mommy, and I only need $37 to go on that trip to Snoqualmie Falls."

Mr. Boppington looked at Buster sternly. "Son, the chances of your ESP being accurate is probably a million to one. We came here today to teach you a lesson. I'm positive that you do not have the ability to pick winning horses and I feel badly that we are spending almost $20 to prove a lesson to you."

Buster was puzzled. "Daddy, what do you mean, we're spending $20? I thought we were betting $2!"

"Son, the admission tickets, the food we have eaten, and a few other charges bring our cost to close to $20. Today we are all going to learn an expensive lesson at the track."

Soon the horses in fifth race had entered the starting gate. Disappointment showed on Mr. and Mrs. Boppington's faces as they saw Puddinhead Putterman's tired body patiently waiting for the gate to open. Buster's was filled with fear — perhaps Nappy had been given the wrong information and the horse his family had bet on was really a loser. Then the gates opened. There were 10 horses in the race, and at the halfway point, Puddinhead Putterman was in very last place. When the race began, Mrs. Boppington felt there was a chance for Buster's horse to win, but as she listened to the half-way results, her confidence vanished. Buster closed his eyes and prayed. Mr. Boppington was smiling, because he thought his son would learn a valuable lesson — that miracles only happen in books and movies.

But then, what seemed like a miracle did happen. Buster's father watched in amazement as, one by one, the horses seemed to slow to a crawl. Angry jockeys snapped their whips on the sides of the animals, but the horses continued to defy their riders. All the horses slowed, that is, except Puddinhead Putterman. Old Puddinhead ran as fast as he possibly could and within 10 seconds he was in front of the pack.

Suddenly the track announcer proclaimed, "And the winner is Puddinhead Putterman, by three lengths." Buster's heart leaped as he heard the results. Mr. Boppington embraced his son and hugged his wife. All three Boppingtons jumped up and down for joy. "We won, we won," squealed a laughing Mr. Boppington.

Mrs. Boppington cashed in the ticket and got almost $300 in cash. It turned out the tote board did not go higher than 99-to-1, but the odds were much higher because almost everyone thought Puddinhead Putterman did not have a chance to win. The actual odds had been almost 150-to-1.

On the way home, Mrs. Boppington told her son that he was to be given $50.00 of the winnings. "Buster," she said, "you can use the money to buy anything you want. My boy, you are truly amazing. One moment you're studying to be a ventriloquist and then I find out you have ESP. Sid, we have a real genius here!"

Mr. Boppington nodded, and Buster saw a wonderful, proud smile on his father's face.

CHAPTER 7
NAPPY SPEAKS OUT

Two weeks had passed since Nappy had miraculously been given the power of human speech. The dog was faithful to Buster's command that he not let anyone else know he could talk.

One evening, just before bedtime, when Nappy and Buster were quietly discussing the day's events, the poodle had an urge for a snack. "Buster, do you remember those delicious dog biscuits you bought me at the store last week?" he asked hopefully.

"You mean those expensive ones. You know, pal, I paid seventy-five cents a package for those, plus tax," Buster sighed.

"Buster, what's a tax?" Nappy asked.

Buster scratched his head and thought about the answer for a moment. "I don't exactly know what tax is, but I have an idea it's money collected to pay for our government to operate. In Washington state, where we live, they even used to charge tax on food." Buster laughed as he said, "Isn't that the most ridiculous thing you ever heard of?"

Buster looked at Nappy expecting him to laugh in agreement. Instead, Nappy had a serious expression on his face, the kind Buster's teachers often had when they were pondering a difficult question. "Buster, you said they don't charge tax on food, but they do charge tax on my treats."

For a moment Buster didn't understand the point Nappy was trying to make. Then he caught on. "You're right, dogs have to eat, just like people do, and if you put a tax on their food it makes it harder for their owners to buy food."

Nappy smiled. "Buster, you're extremely bright, and I'm happy that you're my best friend. Obviously, the ridiculous tax on dog food cannot continue. We have to figure out a way to stop this stupid thing." Nappy stomped his foot on the floor in emphasis.

The following morning at the breakfast table, Buster was eating his oatmeal, his father was sipping his coffee and his mother was talking on the phone to a friend. Buster looked at his father inquisitively. "Dad, why do they charge tax on dog food?"

Mr. Boppington always treated his son's questions with the same respect as an adult's. He thought for a moment. "Son, Washington state considers dogs to be a luxury, something that is not really needed."

"That's crazy," said Buster. "I don't have any brothers or sisters and Nappy's my best friend. He's always here to play with after school and at night I feel safe because I know he'll protect me in case burglars try to break into our house. Daddy, dogs help blind people and they help catch criminals with their sense of smell."

"You know, Buster," said Mr. Boppington, "your reasoning is very logical. I agree that it's unfair to charge tax on dog food."

"Daddy," said Buster, "how do you change the law to get rid of that stupid tax?"

Mrs. Boppington had hung up the phone and joined the discussion. "Senator Hickenbottom is running for re-election. He is going to speak at the school PTA meeting next week," she said. "Buster, maybe Dad and I could take you to the meeting so that you could ask him that question."

That evening Buster excitedly told Nappy that he was going to go to the PTA meeting to try to find out why there was a tax on dog food. Nappy just smiled.

It rained the night of the PTA meeting. When the three Boppingtons arrived at the school auditorium Buster immediately saw Miss Madill. She gave him a stern look, and Buster knew she was wondering why a 10-year-old was at a meeting for adults.

Buster watched as Senator Hickenbottom rose to speak. The senator's shiny bald head seemed to glow under the lights and his overweight body was bulging out of his expensive suit. He took the microphone in his hand and said, "We had a very tough time in the State Legislature passing a good budget. As I have done in years past, I fought for more money for education and better police protection." At this point many people in the audience applauded.

The senator spoke for more than half an hour and many people became bored. Then he suddenly stopped talking and smiled at the audience. "Are there any questions?" he asked.

In the very back of the room, Buster Boppington stood up and said, "I have a question! I have a question!"

Senator Hickenbottom looked at Buster in disbelief and a look of irritation crossed his face. "Yes, young man, what is your question?" the senator asked in a mocking tone.

"Sir," Buster said respectfully, "I have a dog, and couple of days ago I found out that our state charges tax on dog food. Rich people don't have to pay tax on dog food because they can feed their pets hamburger. Why do we have this stupid tax?"

The senator tried to answer, but Buster continued. "I love my dog. He's my best friend and he protects me at night and keeps me company in the day. Why do we have this stupid tax?" When Buster finished, most of the people in the audience applauded.

The senator looked angry. "My young man, a dog is just an animal and don't you ever forget that. Don't ever try to treat them as humans, because they're not. The tax on dog food is a good tax because it helps balance our state's budget. As long as I'm in office I'll continue to support this needed source of revenue."

As the senator finished speaking an amazing event took place. Most of the people in the audience started to boo him and someone yelled out, "Hickenbottom go home! Hickenbottom go home!" Soon almost everybody was yelling "Hickenbottom go home! Hickenbottom go home!"

The following day in math class, Miss Madill came into the room, quietly walked up behind Buster and whispered, "Young man, at the end of this class, would you please come to the office."

As Buster entered the office, he remembered the last time he had been there. It was when he had been late to school and she had been very kind. But Buster was still fearful. He expected to be scolded for being at the PTA meeting.

Miss Madill took her right hand and casually pushed back some of the gray hair from her forehead and then did something that shocked Buster. She laughed heartily. Her face suddenly looked years younger and Buster wondered how he ever could have thought Miss Madill was ugly. "Buster Boppington," she said, "I've been going to PTA meetings for almost 40 years. Usually they're terribly boring affairs, especially the ones where politicians go on and on about all the good they're doing for the school system. Last evening, because you were motivated, you spoke more common sense in two minutes than I've heard in all the other PTA meetings I have attended." As she finished speaking, she put her hands gently on Buster's shoulders.

For a moment Buster did not know what to say. Deep inside he was thrilled. "I'm happy you're not angry at me. Last night and this morning we received a bunch of phone calls from people saying they'll try to defeat Senator Hickenbottom and elect a person against a dog-food tax."

He paused for a moment as an idea raced through his mind. "Miss Madill, why don't you run for the State Senate? In school last week they taught us about a man named Thomas Paine. He wrote a book before the Revolutionary War called *Common Sense*. The book told people that they should do things the right way. Miss Madill, I think that you'd make a great senator. You're smart and you know what our schools need. More than that you know that there should not be a tax on dog food."

Miss Madill was startled. Then she smiled, "You know Buster, rarely do I make snap decisions, but I have made two of them now. Number one, I am going to run against Senator

Hickenbottom, and number two, I want you to assist me with my campaign. You may be only 10, but you seem to have the maturity of a much older person."

Buster's heart leaped for joy.

CHAPTER 8
MISS MADILL RUNS FOR THE SENATE

I n the race for the Senate there were two elections. The first was the primary. The primary was an elimination contest to narrow the field of candidates to two for each office. In the primary, Senator Hickenbottom won 78 percent of the vote. Miss Madill came in second with 19 percent, enough to challenge Senator Hickenbottom in the November final elections.

Two days after the primary, Buster went to Miss Madill's office to congratulate her. "You're half-way there," he said, "you're in the finals."

Miss Madill did not smile. "Buster, I don't have a chance in a million of defeating Hickenbottom," she said, frowning. "He has so much campaign money he could probably defeat the president of the United States."

Buster did not know what to say, but tried to comfort her. "I have a friend who knows a lot about politics. I'll ask him tonight what he thinks you should do."

It was late at night in Buster's room before he had a chance to ask Nappy about Miss Madill's problem. "So you see," Buster said, "there seems to be no way that Miss Madill can win the election. She told me that it takes a lot of money to win and Senator Hickenbottom has lots of it and she has hardly any."

"You mean, the candidate who gets the most money wins the election?" Nappy mused.

"That's what Miss Madill says. I guess they need money to put those stupid commercials on TV." Buster looked at Nappy intently. "Can you think of a way she can win?"

Nappy smiled. "That ought to be easy — tomorrow I'll tell you my plan."

In the morning Buster awoke early to find Nappy waiting for him at the side of the bed. It took his dog only five minutes to describe his victory plan for Miss Madill.

At lunchtime Buster went to Miss Madill's office with renewed enthusiasm. She looked up and smiled. "I spoke to my friend and he thinks he knows how you can win the election," Buster told her. "He said that voters are probably angry at watching the candidates receive a fortune in contributions from the rich people. He also told me that it's not right that the rich people can make the senators do what they want after the election because the senators feel obligated. His plan is for you to campaign on the idea that the regular people should have as much power as the rich. You should tell the voters that you don't want their money, you just want their vote. In our nation, he said, candidates should be elected without strings attached."

Miss Madill smiled widely. "The idea sounds so simple, logical and workable. I wonder though, how I can get the proper news coverage without enough donations."

"My friend told me that the newspapers will be so excited that a candidate is just asking for votes and not for money, they'll make it into a big story. You won't have to buy publicity, you'll get it free," Buster replied.

On November 4th, a saddened Sen. Hickenbottom announced on TV that he was conceding the election to his opponent, Miss Stella Madill. When he was asked by a reporter why he lost the election, he replied, "A stupid 10-year-old kid ruined it for me because I believed that there should be a tax on dog food and he didn't!"

CHAPTER 9
AFTER THE ELECTION

It was a stormy November afternoon when Buster entered Miss Madill's office again. She had become a celebrity overnight. Throughout the state of Washington thousands of voters sent her letters and telegrams of congratulation. They thanked her for not seeking campaign contributions from the wealthy.

As Buster looked at Miss Madill his heart beat rapidly. He knew he was about to be praised for what he had done and somehow he was embarrassed by this. Deep down inside, he felt that it was really his 9-pound talking poodle, Nappy, that deserved all the credit for the miracle election victory. Miss Madill cleared her throat, "Buster I'll soon be taking my place in the Legislature. You and I know that my being elected to the state Senate is because of your fight to stop the unfair taxation on dog food. Furthermore, young man, just when I was about to throw in the towel and quit the race you consulted your friend who is so knowledgeable about politics. His advice that people were tired of having candidates elected with strings attached was the key to my success. I'm sure George Washington and Abraham Lincoln did not have to solicit people's precious dollars to get elected. Those great men just wanted to have the popular vote, which in a democracy is the right of everyone to give without costing a cent."

"Miss Madill, I'm happy you won. The only thing that bothers me is that you'll probably have to leave our school when you go to the Senate."

Miss Madill looked at Buster and chuckled. "Don't worry, Buster, in Washington the job of state Senator is a part-time position. I'll have to take some time off, but I'll be able to keep my regular job. The reason I asked you to come to the office today is to find out if you could someday have your parents bring you to our Capitol so you can watch the real Senate in action."

Buster could not conceal his joy. "You mean," he gushed, "that I'm invited to Olympia to watch the laws being made?" He was beaming from ear to ear.

"Buster," Miss Madill said more seriously, "very soon you'll be old enough to help me in the Legislature. In a couple of years I'll recommend that you become a Senate page."

"What's that?" Buster asked.

"A page is a young person who runs errands for senators. While you're working as a page, you'll be learning how our government works. Young man, I'm so proud of your achievements and thankful for your help that someday soon you're going to have to introduce me to that friend of yours who was so instrumental in helping me win."

When the 3:10 bell rang that day, Buster dashed out of math class and raced home. He was very happy. He wanted to tell his parents and Nappy about his invitation to watch and someday participate in the legislative process.

As Buster ran up his front yard he saw his father's car in the driveway. As his father opened the door of the vehicle, Buster yelled "Hi Daddy," but Mr. Boppington was too preoccupied to acknowledge his son's greeting. Buster instantly realized that his father was upset and asked what was wrong. "I'll tell you later," his father said sadly.

When the family was seated for dinner later, Mrs. Boppington served leg of lamb with mint jelly, one of her husband's favorite meals. Normally, Mr. Boppington would dig in and remark on the excellence of the meal. Today he just pecked at his food.

"What's wrong, dear?" Mrs. Boppington asked tenderly.

Mr. Boppington put down his fork. He ran his fingers through his hair and scratched at his nose. "I went to Boeing to see about my new job. I found out that there is no job. It seems they won't hire me because the bank is putting pressure on the authorities to have me indicted and convicted of stealing the money." As Mr. Boppington finished, tears rolled down his face.

It was nearly 10:30 p.m. before Buster had a chance to talk to Nappy. "So you see," he explained, "things look almost hopeless for Dad. I know he didn't do it, but how can I prove it?"

Nappy did not respond.

Buster looked down at him on the floor and was surprised to see that the pup was already deep asleep. He hopped down and began to gently rub his friend. Nappy slowly and reluctantly awoke. "What is it?" he asked between yawns.

"Nappy," Buster said seriously, "we have to get my father out of all the trouble he's in. We both know he didn't steal that money and all we have to do is prove what we know."

Nappy laughed. "How are we going to do that?"

"You're perhaps the smartest person — I mean smartest something or other — I know. With your keen brain I bet you can find a way to prove Daddy didn't steal the money!"

"Maybe you're right, Buster. Let's talk about it in the morning when I'm awake," Nappy said and happily drifted back to sleep.

Chapter 10
Mr. Boppington Remembers

uster's radio began to play rock 'n' roll at exactly 6:45 in the morning. He sleepily pushed off the covers and gingerly put his feet on the cold hardwood floor. Buster gazed at his sleeping pet, who was sprawled out on the green blanket Mrs. Boppington had given him when he had come to their home. "Nappy! Nappy! It's time to get up," Buster whispered, nudging him gently.

Nappy stretched, gave Buster a sleepy look and slowly began to rise. "You kept me up late last night. I need my sleep to stay healthy and alert," he grumbled.

"Sorry, Nap, but I truly believe there is a good chance we can get Dad out of this mess. Today I'd like you to help me find out who really robbed the bank."

"Buster, we just may be able to find out who the thief is.

I don't know if I told you, but before I moved here, I lived with a police detective. I learned a lot about solving crimes from my previous master."

Buster was amazed. "You mean you were taught how to solve crimes?"

Nappy chuckled. "I mean that when you live in a home where your master is a detective, and if you're an observant dog like I am, you learn a lot about solving crimes."

Buster was adamant. "More than anything in the world I just want to prove that my Dad didn't rob that stupid bank!"

"OK," Nappy said with a smile. "Our search for the real criminal begins today. When you have breakfast, I want you to ask your father every detail of what happened on the Friday of the robbery, and I'll be under the table listening.

And by the way, Buster," Nappy added, "please be a little more careless with your food. There haven't been too many crumbs dropped lately." Buster giggled and got dressed.

At breakfast, Mr. Boppington was just beginning to sip his second cup of coffee when Buster cleared his throat. "Dad I know you have been upset, and I was wondering if there is anything I can do to help you?"

Mr. Boppington regarded his son for a moment. At first his expression was strained, but then, to Buster's relief, his father chuckled. "Son, if you really want your mother and me to feel better, tell me how I can prove to the world that I never stole the money." Again his father laughed.

Buster looked into his father's eyes and Mr. Boppington suddenly noticed a maturity in his boy he had not noticed before.

"Dad, do you remember when I had that dream that I was going to pick a winner at the racetrack?" Mr. Boppington nodded, still smiling. Buster continued, "Last night I had another wonderful dream. It was so real. I asked you all kinds of questions about what happened at the bank on the Friday afternoon that you locked all the money in the vault."

Mrs. Boppington put down her coffee cup and interrupted excitedly: "Buster, did you dream you caught the real crook?"

Buster smiled. "Yes, Mom, I did. I believe it can come true if Daddy can tell me everything that happened the night he locked up the money, and then what happened the morning the money was discovered missing."

Mr. Boppington choked on a piece of toast. It took him a moment to regain his composure. "Buster, that is the most ridiculous notion you have ever come up with. How in heaven's name could you ever think that you could solve this crime?"

Buster was not deterred. He knew he had to convince his father to tell him everything. "Daddy, you're probably right, but you have to admit that my dream did come true for the horse race and don't you think it'd be a good idea to try every way to solve this?"

"Buster," Mr. Boppington said seriously, "I know in my heart that it will do no good, but I also now it will do no harm. I've already gone over every detail with the police and the FBI, so I might as well tell you, too."

Mrs. Boppington looked at her son proudly. "Buster, I have tremendous faith in your abilities. Lately you have been demonstrating so many wonderful talents, like ESP and ventriloquism, and you have grown up a lot. I know you can help."

CHAPTER 11
NAPPY LISTENS

Mr. Boppington nervously reached for his cup and took a giant gulp of coffee. "I remember the day so well," he began. "It was sunny and warm when I arrived at the bank that Friday morning. My spirits were high and I was sure it was going to be a great day. The peculiar thing was, everything did go extremely well that day. For one thing, in all the years that I had been at the bank I never saw Mr. Gonifman crack a smile, but that day he was beaming from ear to ear. He even asked if I could go to lunch with him!"

"Did you go to lunch with him?" Mrs. Boppington asked.

"Well, I wanted to, but I had a dental appointment during my lunch hour. I had already told him about the appointment two weeks before. I always did. I guess he forgot, though he never did before. When I reminded him about it, he just smiled and said we would have to go to lunch very soon. For the next hour I kept wondering why, after all my years at the bank, he suddenly wanted to go to lunch with me.

"About 10:30 I took my coffee break and went to his office. When I rapped on the window, I could see he was thinking 'What the heck are YOU doing here?' I opened his office door and asked if there was something special he had wished to discuss with me at lunch. His frown immediately turned into another rare smile. He then told me something that made my spirits fly: he said he was going to give me a promotion."

"A promotion!" the words burst out of Buster. "Daddy, you mean that on the Friday just before the Monday that you were canned, the boss was going to give you a raise?"

Mr. Boppington was somber. "Not only a raise, but he said he was going to make me a vice president. I was finally going to get some real recognition for my hard work." Mr. Boppington grabbed a napkin and dabbed at a tear.

"After Mr. Gonifman gave me the wonderful news, I was on cloud nine," he said.

"Dad, did anything unusual happen that day, anything that could have caused the money to disappear?" Buster asked.

Mr. Boppington scratched at his face and thought for a moment. "The crazy thing is that I cannot, for the life of me, remember anything else out of the ordinary that day. . . . Oh, wait a second, there WAS one thing. Usually on Fridays old man Floyd, the assistant head teller, and I close up the bank together. But on Thursday Floyd had a minor stroke and I was told he wouldn't be back to work for some time."

"You mean," Mrs. Boppington asked, "that for the first time since you were at the bank you closed the vault by yourself?"

"That's right."

"So, if there had been someone with you, like Floyd, you would have had a witness to your innocence."

Mr. Boppington looked at his feet. "Sweetheart, I've mulled that fact over almost a million times. As fate would have it, I have no witness."

"Dad," Buster pressed, "did you lock the vault?"

"Son, I locked the vault just as I had thousands of times . . . and I know your next question: 'Could someone enter the vault during the weekend and steal the money?' The answer is no. Once I set the time lock, the vault cannot open until 8:30 Monday morning. At precisely 8:30 a.m. Monday, Mr. Gonifman, myself and four tellers marched to the vault together. Mr. Gonifman opened the large safe in the vault and, to everyone's utter astonishment, most of the money was gone."

Mr. Boppington blew his nose with his napkin. "Well son, that's the whole story. Now," he said, smiling weakly, "put your magical powers to work and find the answer to my mystery."

Buster chuckled. "Gee, Dad, even Sherlock Holmes gets a few days to solve his mysteries. I just started this case 20 minutes ago." Everyone laughed at Buster's reply.

When Buster got home from school that day Nappy was home alone. He gave his dog a quick hug and asked, "Nappy, did my Dad tell us anything that will help our investigation."

Nappy smiled smugly. "I got lots of information that would help, but why should I tell you?"

Buster was taken aback. "What d'ya mean? You're my best friend and I'd do anything in the world for you!"

Nappy laughed. "A best friend should drop crumbs on the floor. I'm famished and you want me to go on solving mysteries?"

Buster apologized for his thoughtlessness and soon Nappy was happily chewing on one of his big, tasty dog biscuits. "The most telling clue," he said between mouthfuls, "is that Mr. Gonifman never openly smiled before. Then, suddenly on that Friday, he not only smiles, he offers your father a promotion."

"Nappy, you're right. I thought those two things seemed kind of fishy, too. It also seems queer that these things occurred on the only day that my father ever locked up the vault alone. And another thing," Buster said thoughtfully, "was that Mr. Gonifman asked Dad to lunch on a day that he knew my father had a dental appointment."

Nappy looked at Buster proudly. "You know," he said, "I think you and I would make terrific detectives. After we get your father out of this mess maybe we could try to help other people in trouble."

"That would be great, Nappy, but now we have to concentrate all our efforts on finding out who really stole the money."

Nappy smiled knowingly. "Come, my dear friend, don't you know who probably stole the money? It has to be Gonifman!"

Buster was stunned. "My father's boss?" he gasped.

"I think Gonifman set your father up," Nappy asserted. "You just cited the evidence: Gonifman knew about your father's appointment, therefore, Gonifman knew your father could not go to lunch that day. Why invite someone to lunch when you know they can't go? I'll tell you why. . . to confuse them.

"Furthermore, a man who has acted in one manner for years does not suddenly change his behavior unless something is up. Think about it — all of a sudden old sour-puss Gonifman is all smiles. Buster there are too many coincidences that point to Gonifman. Now," he said with assurance, "the first half of this case is probably solved."

"Probably solved?!" Buster said in disbelief.

"If Gonifman stole the funds," Nappy continued, "there has to be a motive . . . a reason why he committed the crime. Give me a little time and I'll find out what that motive was."

Nappy paused and Buster could see he was concerned. "What's the matter?" he asked.

"The next part," the dog said solemnly, "is the more difficult piece of the puzzle."

"What's that?" Buster asked apprehensively.

"Finding out HOW Gonifman stole the money."

At that moment, Buster and Nappy heard Mrs. Boppington's soft footsteps in the hallway.

Buster motioned for them to be quiet. "We'll talk later," he whispered.

It was almost 11 p.m. before the two crime-solvers had a chance to discuss the investigation again. Nappy was curled up on his blanket and Buster, who had just finished brushing his teeth, was getting into his pajamas. Buster sat on the edge of the bed just as his dog let out a gaping yawn. "I'm pooped," he said as he stretched out the kinks. "I know how important this is, so let's decide what to do tomorrow so I can go to sleep."

Buster was uneasy. "Nappy, I really don't know what to do. I'm all mixed up."

"Don't worry," the dog replied nonchalantly. "Tomorrow I'm going to Gonifman's house."

"What do you think you might find there?" Buster asked.

"Well, the first thing I'll find out is if Gonifman has a dog or a cat."

"You mean you can talk to cats, too?" Buster said with amazement.

"Oh, I've studied a little bit of 'Meow' and I get by with cats fairly well. Naturally, I'd prefer to talk to a dog because it's easier to communicate when there's no language barrier."

"Is there anything I can do to help?" Buster offered.

"No, Buster, you just go to school and cross your fingers for me."

The next morning both Nappy and Buster were extremely tired. Buster's alarm clock was on the fritz again and Mrs. Boppington had to give him two wake-up calls before he managed to get out of bed and stumble to the bathroom.

After Buster was finally off to school, Nappy scratched at the door and Mrs. Boppington let him out. "Hurry back, Nappy, and I'll give you a treat," Mrs. Boppington said with a smile.

Oh, that was a terrible temptation for the always-hungry little dog. "Darn it," he thought, "here I have to go all the way to Gonifman's, almost five miles, just when I'm offered a treat." But he considered the importance of his mission, turned himself against temptation and headed out into the crisp November air.

A cold wind rippled through his thick hair, and he quickened his pace to keep warm. He had gone about two miles when he noticed a large green van. Unfortunately, he didn't notice the small sign on the side of it that read, "County Animal Control."

Suddenly a young man in uniform was heading toward him.

Nappy's first instinct was to keep going on his way, but the man seemed harmless and said sweetly, "Here, pooch. Here, pooch."

On top of that, he had a really nice big dog biscuit in his hand. Nappy knew he shouldn't take food from strangers, but he had already passed up one golden opportunity that morning . . . it was hard to resist.

When Nappy hesitated the man lunged, the dog tried to jump away, but it was too late. A huge net came down around him, and the more he struggled, the more he became entangled. Within moments, he was shoved into a small wire cage in the back of the green van. The next thing he knew, the van was on its way, to the pound, he assumed. "I could kick myself for not wearing a collar," he thought.

The inside of the truck was very dark. When Nappy's eyes adjusted to the dimness he saw that he was surrounded by eight other dogs of various breeds and descriptions. Most were barking incessantly, and the noise was deafening. It was hard to think straight.

A short while later, the van came to a stop and the driver got out. He seemed to be taking a candy break.

The other dogs calmed down a fraction, just enough for Nappy to collect his thoughts. He had to get out, but how? "Think," he thought to himself. "Think hard."

Then an idea came to him. It was brilliant, he thought, mentally patting himself on the back.

He watched the man carefully as he chewed on a candy bar and waited for the right moment.

The next time the dog-catcher stuffed the candy in his mouth, he yelled in a high, shrill voice that sounded like a child, "Help me, help me. I'm only 5 years old and my mommy will get mad when she finds out what you've done to me." The dog-catcher looked around in disbelief. Nappy went on, "Please let me out, these dogs back here are so scary."

When the dog-catcher heard this, he swallowed the whole

candy bar, bit his tongue and began to cough and choke uncontrollably. At the same time, he was so overcome with fear that a child had somehow been locked up with one of the dogs that he jumped into the back of the van and began opening cages to find the youngster.

Nappy's prison was the fourth one opened. Just before he leaped to the street he whimpered, "Please let me go. Please let me go." The man opened the rest of the cages in his frantic, vain search for the child, freeing all the dogs in the process.

Nappy hid in some nearby bushes almost 30 minutes till the coast was clear. Because of the unfortunate delay it took him almost three hours to get to Mr. Gonifman's beautiful sprawling home.

The first thing he noticed was that Gonifman had an expensive lifestyle. There was a new Mercedes in the driveway and the front yard obviously was maintained by a professional gardener. Everything smelled of money and Nappy knew bankers did not make as much money as people assumed they did. He began to suspect that Mr. Gonifman was living higher on the hog than his salary allowed.

Nappy also knew whether there was a dog or cat pet in residence. His superb sense of smell could not be questioned. He instantly realized that Gonifman had no pets.

Tired and disappointed, he sprawled out in a secluded corner of the yard to catch his breath and figure out what to do next.

The harsh sound of a dog barking abruptly awakened the dozing private eye a short while later. Nappy rubbed his eyes with his paw to clear his vision. First he looked right, then left, to find the source of the bark. Finally he spotted a beautiful brown-and-white toy collie pup at the far end of the lawn.

Nappy approached the beautifully groomed dog cautiously, not wishing to seem aggressive. "Hi, what's your name," he called out casually.

"Rex Trudeau," the pup replied. "I live in the white house on the corner."

"You mean," Nappy said, trying to hold back his excitement, "that you live next door to the Gonifmans?"

Rex smiled proudly. "I've lived here all of my life. In fact, I was born in that house almost six months ago."

Nappy smiled back and poured on the charm. "Gee, Rex, I thought you were much older than six months. You have that mature look about you, not at all like a puppy."

Rex, happy that someone was treating him like a grownup, broke into a smile. "Gee, it sure is nice to see a friendly face. Around here there aren't any friendly animals. There's a mean pit bull that lives about a block away and a stuck-up basset hound that won't even speak to me. By the way, Mister, I didn't get your name?"

"I'm Napoleon Boppington, but you can call me Nappy. I live about five miles from here."

Rex whistled in amazement. "Boy, you've come a long way. Are you exercising or are you in my neighborhood for a reason?"

Nappy decided not to mince words. "Rex, I'm here on a mission. I am positive that Mr. Gonifman has robbed a bank . . . his own bank, and I'm trying to prove it."

Rex was taken aback at first, then, gradually, he loosened up. "I can tell you terrible things about Mr. Gonifman," he said. "He's a thief."

Nappy's tail wagged with excitement. "Tell me what you mean," he said.

"Well, I'm not talking about a bank robbery here," Rex

said, "but there's something he does that really irks me. About a block from here there's a newspaper machine that carries the morning paper. About two weeks ago I watched Gonifman as he put a quarter in the machine, opened the glass door and, then, instead of taking out one paper, he took at least three. The first time I saw him do it, I thought he was in a hurry and had made a mistake. After he did the same thing every day for an entire week, I knew Gonifman was no more than a common thief."

Nappy now moved in for the kill. "Rex, has Gonifman shown any signs lately of coming into a big sum of money?"

Rex scratched his head thoughtfully. "No, I haven't seen anything that would point to that."

"Darn it!" Nappy said. His disappointment could not be mistaken.

But Rex seemed not to hear Nappy. "If anything, I'd say he's having money problems," the pup said.

"Aha!" Nappy exclaimed. "That makes perfect sense. If Gonifman has financial problems, that would be the motive for robbing the bank. Tell me, Rex, what makes you think he's in debt?"

"One evening about two weeks ago, I was resting on the lawn, feeling the cool grass on my tummy. Shortly after dark, a black limousine pulled into the Gonifman's driveway. There were two well-dressed men in the back seat, one of whom got out and knocked at Gonifman's door. Mrs. Gonifman answered and asked the man what he wanted. He asked for Mr. Gonifman, who came outside. The porch light was on and I could see Gonifman — he was pale and shaky."

"The next thing you know," Rex continued, "the well-dressed man told Gonifman that if he didn't have the dough by tomorrow, he'd 'better learn how to swim at the bottom of

Lake Washington.' Gonifman assured the man, over and over, that he would have $10,000 by the next day."

Nappy then asked Rex if he had then actually seen Gonifman hand over the money.

"No," Rex said, "but about a week later the same car returned and the same man asked for money again. Gonifman told the man not to worry, though Gonifman looked terribly worried himself."

Nappy thanked his new friend for the information. As he ambled home, he felt confident he was getting closer to proving that Gonifman robbed the bank. On the other hand, he felt, deep down inside, that proving Mr. Boppington's innocence beyond a shadow of a doubt was still a long way off.

CHAPTER 12
THE DISCUSSION

It was just after midnight, when his parents were finally asleep, before Buster had a chance to discuss the day's events with his friend. "Nappy, Nappy," he whispered. The dog was completely bushed, and, as usual, he was spread out on his blanket in deep sleep. Buster lifted one of Nappy's ears and asked, a little louder, "Nappy, Nappy, are you sleeping?"

The dog awoke like he was jump-started and said sarcastically, "I wasn't sleeping, I was just going to try out for an acting part for anyone who needs a dog who can act like he's asleep. Jeepers, Buster, of course I was sleeping. Don't you know why I'm so tired? Today, without any food, I walked 10 miles and, to top it off, I was arrested by what you humans so pleasantly call the Humane Society. Fortunately for you, I escaped thanks to my superior intelligence."

"Nappy, I beg your pardon. Had I known what happened,

I wouldn't have gotten you up. But I couldn't wait any longer to find out what you learned. You know how much I want to get my Dad out of the jam he's in, and you're really the only chance I have to save him."

Nappy looked at Buster with big, brown tender eyes. He stood up on his hind legs and stroked Buster's face gently with a front paw. "You know, pal," he said soothingly, "that I'd do anything in the world to help your father.

"So here's what I discovered today: I'm almost certain that Mr. Gonifman is a gambler. It looks like he owes his soul to the bookies."

"What's a bookie?" Buster asked innocently.

Nappy looked at Buster for a moment, a little surprised at the boy's naivete. "Do you remember when your parents took you to the track and bet on the horses?" he asked.

"Of course I remember," Buster replied. "It was quite a day."

"The racetrack is where you can legally bet on the horses," Nappy explained. "Now, if you want to place an illegal bet, you go to a bookie, who is a criminal. With a bookie you can bet on just about any sport — baseball, football, horses . . ."

"Nappy", Buster said excitedly, "you said you thought Gonifman was in trouble with the bookies. Explain!"

"Well, Buster, if we assume that Gonifman made a bet over the phone with a bookie and then did not pay up on the bet when he lost, the bookie could not get his money by suing him or reporting him to the police because the bet was illegal."

"Oh, I get it," Buster said. "If Gonifman didn't pay, the only way the bookie might get his money is to threaten to beat him up."

"That's right," Nappy continued. "If Gonifman owed

money to the bookies, that would be an incentive to rob his own bank. So, we have the probable motive, now we need to figure out part two of this puzzle — how he framed your father."

Buster felt a small sense of relief — pieces of the puzzle were starting to fall into place — and he and Nappy soon drifted off to sleep.

When Buster awoke the next morning, his bedroom was a bit chilly. He crawled out from under the covers but when his feet met the cold floor, he dashed for the thermostat in the hall and turned up the heat. Within a short time the Boppington house was a toasty 70 degrees.

The heat and the aromas of breakfast soon woke Nappy, too. Buster opened the front door and let the dog out for his usual morning stroll.

A few minutes later Buster was seated at the breakfast table, where his mother had just placed a big bowl of Cheerios and milk for her son. Buster dug into his cereal when he heard his father's heavy footsteps coming down the hall. "Good morning, Dad," Buster said with a smile.

For a moment it seemed that Mr. Boppington was lost in thought and didn't hear his son's greeting. But then he smiled at Buster and said, "Well, well, how is my son with the ESP doing today?"

Buster blushed. "Dad, I think I'm getting close to solving this crime. I know who probably stole the money and I can tell you right now who it is."

"You can . . . you can . . . ," Mr. Boppington tried to get the words out, but no matter how much he tried, he just stammered.

A loud bark at the door brought his speech back. "Buster," he said, "go let Nappy in first."

When Buster opened the door, Nappy looked up at him and whispered, "Brrr. It's freezing out here. I sure wish you'd let me use the bathroom."

Buster ignored Nappy's complaint and whispered back, "I was just telling my father about Gonifman."

"You what?" Nappy yelled so loudly that even Mrs. Boppington, who was washing dishes, heard him.

She turned to her husband and said, "Isn't it wonderful? Buster can throw his voice just like a professional ventriloquist."

Buster cupped his hand over Nappy's mouth and whispered, "Quiet! Do you want to get me in trouble?"

"No, Buster, I don't," Nappy whispered back, "but if you tell your father that Gonifman robbed the bank before we have total proof, he'll think you're crazy and then you'll be in real trouble."

Buster thought about that for a moment. "I guess you're right. I just wasn't thinking."

"Buster . . . Buster," Mrs. Boppington called, "please come finish your breakfast."

Buster returned to the table and nibbled at his cereal, which had gotten a little soggy. He became aware of his father's gaze and nonchalantly brought his eyes up to meet his father's. It was apparent his Dad was waiting for the rest of the story. "Daddy," he said cautiously, "I really think I know who stole the money, but before I find out all the details, I'm going to need some time."

With a hint skepticism Mr. Boppington said, "Son, I'm beginning to believe that only a miracle can save me. I can't figure out a way to prove I'm innocent."

Buster tried to be encouraging. "Daddy, I promise you I'm going to help find out who stole the money."

Mr. Boppington rose, went over to Buster and gave his son a great big hug.

"I love you so much, Buster, and you know, maybe you're right, because suddenly deep down in my heart I feel that things will get better for our family."

When Buster arrived home from school that afternoon, Nappy was at the door waiting for him. "Your Mom and Dad are at the grocery store, so we need to plan our next move before they get home."

"I can hardly wait," Buster said eagerly. "All day in school I was wondering what we could do next."

"I've been watching an old black-and-white detective show called 'Perry Mason,' " Nappy said. "You know, Buster, that Mason was quite a guy."

Buster was a little annoyed. "You mean you spent all day watching TV instead of trying to help my father."

"That's just the point," Nappy said excitedly, "Perry Mason gave me some great ideas. The first thing we have to do is find out everything we can about Gonifman. We need to know what he was doing from the time he was in grade school until the present."

"That's an awful tall order to fill, Nappy. How would we do that?" Buster asked.

"There are lots of ways to find out information about people," Nappy said. "Let me give you an example: I phoned the Gonifman house this afternoon and said I was from the newspaper. I told Mrs. Gonifman the paper was doing a feature story on successful bankers and I understood that her husband was such a man."

"Nappy, that wasn't honest," Buster scolded.

"You're right, and I felt badly about misrepresenting myself, but I don't think I broke any laws since I didn't tell Mrs.

Gonifman what newspaper I was with and, furthermore, with your dad's electric typewriter, why couldn't I put out a paper? Someday I hope they invent a typewriter for dogs."

"Nappy, you're stretching the point, but I guess since we're trying to get Dad out of trouble, it's OK."

"Buster, I found out many things from my interview. For instance, Mr. Gonifman was a star quarterback at his Jr. high school and, according to his wife, he loved sports more than anything in the world. He had planned to play football in high school when something terrible happened: He was in an automobile accident, his legs were injured and he was in a coma for over a week. He never played football again."

"Gee," Buster wondered, "how does that help us?"

"Detective work is mainly gathering a lot of facts," Nappy explained. "It's like the jigsaw puzzle that you were doing a couple of days ago. You get all the pieces and then try to make them fit. Buster, tomorrow I want you to go to Garfield High School, where Gonifman graduated from. You need to look at the 1960 yearbook and find out everything you can about him. Then talk to any teachers who can remember what kind of a kid Gonifman was."

"Nappy, I guess you know I'll have to skip school to do this," Buster pointed out.

"I don't think missing school for a day will be too great a sacrifice to help prove your father's innocence." As Nappy finished speaking they heard a key turn in the front door. The two detectives made a sign that they would talk later just before Mr. and Mrs. Boppington came into the living room.

CHAPTER 13
BUSTER GOES TO HIGH SCHOOL

Buster arrived at Garfield High School at 9:30 in the morning. As he opened one of the big front double doors of the school, his nostrils were greeted by the musty odor of old books and gym shorts. He strolled down the hall nervously, wondering which way to go.

"May I help you, young man?" The voice came from a tall, gray-haired man who appeared to be about 60 years old. The man had a pleasant smile.

"I'm here to find out information," Buster said, smiling at the gentleman, though his voice gave away his nervousness.

The man chuckled. "Young man, if you want a high school education, it would be prudent of you to graduate from elementary school first."

"Sir, I'm not here to go to class," Buster said, his heart beating rapidly. "I've come to find out information about a student who went here a long, long time ago."

The man chuckled again. "I see," he said, "I guess you must be some kind of Sherlock Holmes and are involved in a big investigation." The man began to laugh hilariously, but just as quickly as he laughed, he stopped when he saw that Buster had burst into tears. The tall man put his hands on Buster's shoulders and gently guided him into a vacant study hall.

He sat Buster down and said, "Young man, I apologize for laughing at you. Obviously, you have a problem and, if you'll tell me what it is, perhaps I can be of assistance."

Buster wiped the tears from his cheeks. "Sir, I probably should not be telling you this, but you seem like a very nice man. My father is in deep trouble. He has lost his job at the bank because of a robbery. Almost everyone seems to think my Dad was the thief, but my best friend and I think the robber is the manager of the bank, a Mr. Gonifman. My friend says that for me to prove Mr. Gonifman is guilty, I should first find out all I can about him, and I've started here because I know he went to Garfield in the 1950s."

The gentleman let out a long whistle. "Young man, you certainly are carrying a big burden, and perhaps if you'll sit here and calm down for a while, I can help. First of all," he asked Buster, "what is Mr. Gonifman's first name?"

"I don't know that," Buster replied, "but I do know that he was in 12th grade at this school in 1960."

The man told Buster to sit still and left the room. A few minutes later he returned with a book under his arm.

"You may be looking for Thomas Gonifman," the man said. "He attended Garfield from 1957 to 1960." He handed the book to Buster. "Here, look in here and see if you can find his picture."

Buster flipped through the thick annual. On Page 34 the picture of a Thomas Gonifman seemed to jump out at him.

Buster felt an eerie chill. The eyes of the young Gonifman in the photo gave him the creeps. "How'd you know where to find his picture?" he asked.

The gentleman smiled. "When you gave me the year he attended Garfield, I simply looked up the senior class for that year. Thomas Gonifman was the only student named Gonifman at Garfield in the 1950s. In 1960, I was teaching at Franklin High School. I did not come to Garfield until 1965."

"Sir," Buster asked anxiously, "are there any teachers here who might remember what Mr. Gonifman was like when he went to Garfield?"

The man was silent for a moment, rubbing his chin in thought. Then he snapped his fingers. "Spritzer! Cyrus Spritzer! He came to Garfield back in '53. Young man, if anyone would know about your Mr. Gonifman, it would be Spritzer."

Buster had to wait two hours before he could meet with Mr. Spritzer, who taught chemistry. Mr. Spritzer was short, fat and bald. His wrinkled face told Buster he was very old.

"Sir," he said politely, "I'm sorry to bother you, but back in 1960 a boy named Thomas Gonifman attended this school. Do you remember him?"

Spritzer massaged his bare scalp with long finger nails. Buster could tell he was searching through memories of thousands of students. After what seemed like forever, he looked at Buster with slightly clouded eyes. "I remember the lad well. He was not a very good student and he often was teased by the others. They had a nickname for him." Spritzer put his index finger to his forehead as he tried to remember the name. "Ah," he said softly, "I remember now. It was 'Gonifman the Wise.' I never understood why they called him that. He rarely got higher than 'C' grades and he flunked my chemistry course."

"Maybe he was always making wisecracks and that's how he got his nickname," Buster offered. It seemed like Mr. Spritzer gave Buster the kind of look that said 'Children should be seen and not heard.' Buster looked down at his feet. "I'm sorry. I guess it was a stupid idea."

"To the contrary, my boy, all scientific discoveries have come from the testing of ideas. In this particular case your hypothesis is not correct. Gonifman was pretty quiet. You know, I remember now that he did have a hobby that occupied much of his time, but I can't for the life of me think of what it was."

Suddenly an ear-shattering bell cracked the silence, and several hundred students stampeded out of their classes for lunch.

When the noise died down, Mr. Spritzer added, "I think that's all I can remember about Thomas Gonifman, except for one thing . . . I never liked him. There was just something about him that troubled me and most of the other people who knew him. Somehow he seemed to care more about himself than anyone else. To put it bluntly, he was selfish."

Buster left the school feeling troubled. On the one hand it was good that he had been able to learn something about Mr. Gonifman, but he was worried that it would be of no help in his father's case.

Chapter 14

Buster Tells Nappy What He Found at Garfield

U sually it was Nappy who was tired and did not want to discuss the day's events. But this evening it was Buster who was completely bushed and it took a great amount of effort to stay awake long enough to give Nappy the results of his investigation. "I didn't find out very much about Gonifman," he conceded sadly.

Nappy scratched his neck. "Buster, anything you learned could be very important. Just tell me the facts and I'll determine whether they're valuable. By the way, I watched a terrific 'Perry Mason' today. . . also a 'Rockford Files' and a 'Barnaby Jones.' From all the education I'm getting, I really think that I would make a wonderful detective."

"OK, OK," Buster said between yawns. "His name is Thomas — his first name that is. He went to Garfield from

1957 until 1960. His chemistry teacher, Mr. Spritzer, told me that hardly anyone liked him." That was all he could tell.

"OK, what else," Nappy prodded.

"Gee, Nap, that's about all that I can think of. I told you there wasn't that much information." Buster could see Nappy's disappointment and he felt a sinking sensation in his stomach. Then, one more fact leapt into his mind. "You know, there was one peculiar thing. The other students nicknamed him 'Gonifman the Wise.' What's funny about it, according to Mr. Spritzer, is that he was not a good student. I asked Mr. Spritzer if he was always making wisecracks and that's how he got his nickname."

"What did Spritzer say?"

"He said it was a good guess, but I was wrong." Buster paused in deep thought. "You know, there *was* one other thing . . . Mr. Spritzer said Gonifman had a hobby, but he couldn't remember what it was." Buster looked down at Nappy sadly. "I told you, pal, I didn't find out very much. It looks almost hopeless, doesn't it?"

"The trouble with you, Buster," Nappy said teasingly, "is that you don't watch enough good television." He giggled and Buster felt better. "Seriously, though," Nappy continued, "you need to remember not to overlook the smallest detail. A fact that may not seem important to us now, may be the detail that can solve this case."

Buster yawned again. "Nappy, I'm really beat, but tell me what our next move should be?"

"My friend, tomorrow is going to be a day to relax and go over all the information we've gathered. I feel confident that we are getting close to a solution. We just need to put the pieces of the puzzle in the proper order so we can find the answer." As Nappy finished he heard Buster snoring lightly.

Chapter 15
The Indictment

"Buster . . . Buster, wake up you sleepyhead. You don't want to be late to school, do you?" his mother called gently from the doorway.

"I'm getting up right now, Mom," he mumbled drowsily. "Don't worry, I'll get to school on time," he assured her as he rolled over and peeked down at Nappy. Buster kind of envied his pet because Nappy didn't have to go to school and could watch TV most of the day.

Nappy stretched and smiled at Buster. "While you're in school I'm going to go over the facts again and again," he whispered. "I just know we have enough clues to solve this thing." He scratched his ear and looked around the room with his big brown eyes.

The quiet moment was pierced by the loud ring of the doorbell. Nappy and Buster both wondered who would be calling at 6:45 a.m. They listened intently as Mrs. Boppington answered the door and heard the deep voice of a man saying, "Ma'am, I'm sorry to bother you so early, but I'm delivering important government documents. Is this the Sidney Boppington residence?"

"Yes, it is," Mrs. Boppington said nervously. "What kind of documents?"

The man replied, "I need to speak to Mr. Boppington, ma'am. Is he home?"

By this time Mr. Boppington had come to the door to see who could possibly be calling at such a ridiculous hour. "How may I help you," he asked the man suspiciously.

"Sir," the man replied gravely, "I am a federal marshal. Last Friday a federal grand jury indicted you on charges of bank robbery."

Mrs. Boppington burst into tears and her husband was frozen in shock.

"Sir," the man continued, "you are to stand trial for a crime. May I remind you that you are innocent until proven guilty. Please sign this receipt for these documents and I'll be on my way."

By this time Buster and Nappy were at Buster's window and watched, stunned, as the man hurried down the walk and jumped into a U.S. marshal's car.

Buster was beside himself. He suddenly felt as if there was nothing he could do to help. He raced to his parents and, with tears welling up in his eyes, gave his father a huge hug. His father hugged Buster back. He then hugged his tearful mother and for a moment the Boppington family felt a little better because they each knew that even if they had nothing else, they had each other's love.

Although Buster was distraught, he went to school that day. Just before lunch his teacher got a note and called Buster.

"Miss Madill would like to see you in her office. She said to come in during the lunch hour."

Soon Buster was standing in front of Miss Madill. Unlike their last meeting, when Miss Madill had just won the election and was all smiles, today she was frowning. "Young man," she began, "I am concerned about you. Your grades are falling again and yesterday you had an unexcused absence."

For a moment Buster was silent. He didn't know what to say. But then his distress got the better and he lost control. His eyes filled with tears as he blurted out, "Miss Madill, this morning my Dad was indicted for bank robbery and he might have to go to prison."

Miss Madill put her strong arms on Buster's shoulders and in a soothing voice said, "Young man, I know you've been living through a terrible nightmare. Perhaps if you tell me what's been going on I could be of some help."

Buster looked at Miss Madill through his tears and began to tell her everything about the past few weeks. Every detail, that is, except for the fact that when he referred to his best friend, Miss Madill assumed he was speaking about a human being instead of a talking dog. "So you see, Miss Madill, I just know Mr. Gonifman stole the money. I know why he stole the money, but I don't know how he did it."

"Buster, you told me before that you skipped class to go to Garfield High School to find out about Gonifman."

Buster's face reddened. "I know it was wrong but my friend told me it would help my father."

Miss Madill smiled. "Son, I'm not angry at you anymore for cutting class. If I were in your shoes, I would have done the same thing. Tell me, what did you find out about Gonifman?"

"Well," Buster said through sniffles, "he went to Garfield from 1957 until 1960 and the other kids called him 'Gonifman The Wise.' "

"Why," Miss Madill asked.

"I don't know, that. Neither did the teacher I talked to, Mr. Spritzer. I asked him if Gonifman was smart and he said he was a lousy student. I asked him if Gonifman was a wiseguy and he said he was very quiet."

"Buster, there is usually a reason for everything," Miss Madill said. "I think I can find out how Gonifman earned the nickname. OK, what else did you learn?"

"About all Mr. Spritzer told me was he never really liked Gonifman and that Gonifman had an unusual hobby, though he couldn't remember what it was."

Miss Madill put her index finger to her chin. "You know, a hobby could be very important in finding out about someone's character. I might be able to help you with that too."

Just then, the bell signaling the end of lunch hour rang.

"Now," she said jovially, "you'd better get to spelling class and leave this part of the investigation up to me."

Chapter 16
Nappy Speaks With Miss Madill

Buster was in math class when Miss Madill learned the answers to the two questions and decided she'd better call Mr. and Mrs. Boppington immediately. The phone rang nine times before Nappy decided to answer it. He pushed the phone off the table with his front paws and the phone hit the floor with a crack. Miraculously, the headset landed face up. "Hello," he said.

"Hello, is this Mr. Boppington?" Miss Madill asked.

Nappy coughed nervously and paused, trying to figure out what to say. He decided it was best to be truthful. "This is the Boppington residence, but I'm not Mr. Boppington."

"Oh," Miss Madill said, "you must be Buster's friend, the gentleman who had the brilliant ideas for my campaign."

Nappy smiled proudly. "Thank you for the compliment and, yes, I'm Buster's best friend."

Miss Madill chuckled. "You know, in all the time that I have spoken to Buster, I never found out your name. What is it?"

"Napoleon," he replied without hesitation.

"Oh, my," Miss Madill exclaimed. "So you're a French gentleman."

Nappy chuckled, "I guess you could say that."

"Well," Miss Madill said, "I have important information for you to pass on to Mr. Boppington. I found out why Mr. Gonifman was called 'Gonifman the Wise' and what his unusual hobby was when he was in high school."

But just as Miss Madill was about to clear up the two mysteries, Nappy heard the back door shut and looked up to find Mrs. Boppington standing in the doorway holding a sack of groceries.

Nappy looked at her and then at the phone sheepishly. Mrs. Boppington assumed the dog had been naughty and scolded him for getting on the table as she picked up the phone, hung up and put it back on the table.

Nappy scampered out of the room, relieved that his secret was still safe, but anxious because he still didn't know the answers to the Gonifman questions. Now he'd have to wait for Buster to get home.

Chapter 17
House For Sale

When Buster arrived home he was startled to see a man pounding a blue-and-white sign into the ground at the end of his sidewalk. The sign said in great big red letters, "FOR SALE."

"Mom, Mom, where are you?" he yelled as he raced into the house.

Mrs. Boppington met Buster in the living room and motioned for him to sit on the couch. She took his hands and rubbed them gently. "Sweetheart," she said as tears welled up in her eyes, "you and I both know that Daddy did not commit a crime. But in order for him to get the best of lawyers, we need money, lots of it. So Daddy and I decided to sell the house."

Buster tried to hold back his tears. He had lived here for most of his 10 years and he loved his home. "Mom, isn't there some way that we can stay in our house?"

Mrs. Boppington at first looked at Buster seriously, then laughed light-heartedly. "There's only one way for us to keep our home: if my 10-year-old boy uses his miraculous ESP to find the real thief."

Buster felt very badly because, unlike his mother, he knew he didn't have ESP.

At this moment, Nappy burst into the room and began to paw at Buster excitedly. Buster looked into his dog's big brown eyes and knew Nappy had to talk to him. "Mom, it looks like Nappy needs to go out, so I'll take him to the back yard," he said and headed for the kitchen door.

When they got outside Nappy told Buster about his conversation with Miss Madill. "You need to call her back right away," he said.

When Miss Madill answered her phone, Buster said, "Hello Miss Madill, I need the answers to the two puzzles?" After a while he hung up the phone and looked at Nappy. His face was flushed with excitement. "Quick," he said, "let's go to my room — we have work to do!"

Buster whispered the information to Nappy as the dog's tail wagged wildly. "So now," Buster concluded, "we probably know how the money disappeared and why Gonifman was called 'Gonifman the Wise.' " Buster paused and scratched his forehead. "We're so close to solving this mess, where do we go from here?"

"Buster, fortunately I've watched so many mysteries on TV that I know exactly what we have to do — get Gonifman to confess."

"How?" Buster asked.

"It shouldn't be that difficult but I'll have to sleep on it," Nappy said with a wink.

CHAPTER 18
BUSTER BOPPINGTON DETECTIVE

The next day, the Tuesday before Thanksgiving, Nappy filled Buster in on his plan. "We have to contact the police or the FBI and tell them everything we know." "How are we going to get them to believe us," Buster worried. "If I go to the police they'll probably ignore me — and YOU certainly can't go!"

"Well, you're right, there," Nappy replied, "but why don't you ask Miss Madill for help."

Buster phoned Miss Madill again. "Stella Madill, may I help you?"

"Miss Madill, this is Buster Boppington and I . . ."

"Why, Buster, I've been hoping to hear from you. Is there anything more I can do for you?"

Buster took a big gulp. "Miss Madill because of your help, my friend and I have solved the riddle. We know how the money was stolen, but now we have to prove it to the police. The problem is, that if I go to the police they won't take me seriously because I'm a kid."

"Wait a minute, Buster," Miss Madill interrupted him. "I have a cousin who is a Seattle police captain and he's a very understanding man who loves children. Just tell me what I can do."

Later that day Buster phoned Miss Madill's cousin, Capt. Philips. He told the police officer the details of the crime his father was accused of and why he thought Mr. Gonifman was the real thief.

Capt. Philips was very friendly and told Buster he would launch a new investigation.

The phone rang during dinner that evening. Mr. Boppington answered it. "Hello . . . yes, I'm Sidney Boppington." Buster watched his father's face. At first he looked concerned but when he hung up the phone his expression had changed to one of relief.

"Who was that Sid?" Mrs. Boppington asked hopefully.

"That was Seattle Police Capt. Philips. He wants you, me and Buster to be at Gonifman's bank tomorrow morning at 7 sharp. He has new evidence in the robbery and says he thinks I'm innocent."

The Boppingtons just looked at each other through tears of joy.

Buster awoke the following morning at 5:30 with a great sense of hope. Tomorrow would be Thanksgiving. He went to his window and looked out at the frost-covered grass. His room was chilly as usual, but he didn't seem to notice.

Nappy yawned and whispered, "If all goes well today, we'll have an incredible Thanksgiving celebration tomorrow."

Buster smiled at his friend and nodded. He was too happy for words.

CHAPTER 19
THE MEETING

"What's going on here?" a surprised Mr. Gonifman snarled as he arrived at the bank to find the Boppingtons waiting at the door. "Sid, what are you all doing here? Under the circumstances, it's not very wise," he sneered.

Before Mr. Boppington could answer, a police car pulled up to the bank. Two officers got out and identified themselves to Gonifman. "I'm Officer Hendriques and this is Captain Philips. We're here to investigate the recent robbery."

Gonifman nervously scratched his face and growled, "What's going on? The investigation has already been concluded."

Capt. Philips ignored Gonifman. "What time does the vault unlock?" he asked.

Mr. Gonifman coughed. "Not until 8:30 sharp."

"Please unlock the door and let us in," Philips continued.

Gonifman looked at the Boppingtons and said, "I'll let you two officers in the bank but the man over there stole almost $100,000. Why should I let him in?"

Capt. Philips addressed Gonifman sternly. "We will all enter the bank, including Mr. Boppington."

By 8:15 the bank employees had arrived for work and were whispering among themselves about the presence of the police and the Boppingtons.

At 8:30 Buster heard a big click and watched as one of the tellers pulled the heavy steel vault door open. The vault was really just a big storage room. At the far end was a large safe.

Capt. Philips looked at Gonifman and asked, "Now, please show me how you discovered the funds missing on that Monday morning several months ago."

Gonifman cleared his throat a couple of times. Beads of perspiration were rolling down his forehead. "Officer, can you tell me what in blazes is going on here? I can't for the life of me understand why you've brought Sidney Boppington, a thief, to my bank?" He was obviously stalling.

Capt. Philips replied, "We're here today to discover how the money disappeared. Hopefully, Mr. Gonifman, this investigation will just take a few moments and we'll be on our way. Now, please show us how you discovered the money missing."

Gonifman laughed nervously. "I'll be most happy to comply. Please follow me into the vault."

As Gonifman outlined the events, Capt. Philips interrupted, "So on that Monday morning you discovered that almost 80 percent of the paper money in the safe had been stolen."

"That's right." Gonifman answered.

"And Mr. Gonifman," Capt. Philips continued, "is it true that at the time of the disappearance only you and Mr. Boppington had the combination to the safe?"

"That's right. Only myself and Sid Boppington had the combination. But Boppington closed the vault by himself the previous Friday and I'm sure he'll tell you that all the money was in the safe then and it wasn't until Monday morning that I discovered that it had disappeared."

Capt. Philips looked right at Gonifman and repeated, "Disappeared, you say, disappeared? Almost like magic?"

"That's right," Gonifman said.

"Well, according to the original police report, Mr. Boppington said you told him, 'We don't believe in magic here.'"

"What are you getting at?" Gonifman screeched.

Capt. Philips remained calm. "When you went to high school you were known as 'Gonifman the Wise' . . . would you mind telling me why?"

Gonifman's face turned red and he was shaking. "It's been so many years ago, I don't think I can remember," he said.

Capt. Philips looked at the Boppingtons. "The great magician Houdini's real name was Harry Weiss, pronounced 'Wise.' Mr. Gonifman's hobby in his youth was practicing the art of illusion. He was called 'Gonifman the Wise' because he imitated Houdini in his magic acts."

Mrs. Boppington looked at Capt. Philips, somewhat puzzled. "Are you trying to say the money disappeared because of a magic trick."

"That's right. When your husband closed the safe in the vault that Friday it looked like it was filled with money. But Mr. Gonifman had already removed most of the bills and piled the remainder in the front of the safe to give the illusion that it was full. There was no reason for Mr. Boppington to check the rear of the safe because it looked as it had thousands of times in the past.

"When the safe was opened Monday morning, Gonifman immediately shoved the money down to show that most of it was gone."

"That's ridiculous," Gonifman sneered. "You have no proof that I stole the money. You're just guessing how it may have been done."

Capt. Philips chuckled. "Mr. Gonifman, we have enough proof to send you to prison for many years. Two days after the money disappeared you opened 18 new bank accounts. In each one, you deposited $5,000 in 20-dollar bills — exactly the denominations that were stolen. We know this because all bank accounts are tracked by Social Security numbers, and while you may have used different names on these accounts, you used the same Social Security number for them."

Gonifman was caught and he knew it. He suddenly looked frail and old to Buster, not powerful and proud like he used to. "I stole the money," Gonifman admitted, "because I had to. The bookies would have killed me."

Officer Hendriques immediately put handcuffs on Gonifman and read him his rights.

Capt. Philips turned to the Boppingtons. "We never would have solved this case without Buster's work," he said. "When he gets older, I'd sure like to talk to him about a job on the police force."

Buster's parents hugged and kissed him. They were smiling . . . and crying.

CHAPTER 20
THANKSGIVING

Buster awoke early Thanksgiving Day to find two big brown eyes staring at him affectionately. "Well, Buster," Nappy whispered, "things are looking up in our home. Happy Thanksgiving."

Buster smiled, "You know, Nappy, if my Uncle Morrie hadn't sent me that chemistry set, my father would still be in a heap of trouble."

"You're right, Buster, but in the future let's be more careful about experimenting with chemicals. Instead of a talking dog, you could have had a very sick dog, or worse."

"Fear not," Buster promised, "I'll never mix chemicals in your bowl again. Umm, what's that wonderful smell?"

Nappy sniffed deeply. "It smells like a luscious roast turkey. Let's go see."

Nappy and Buster found Mrs. Boppington bending over the oven door basting a big golden-brown bird. She looked up at Buster and smiled. "My son, I'm so proud of you for figuring out the truth about Gonifman. You saved our family."

Buster looked down at Nappy and back at his mother. "Mom," he admitted, "I had help with my investigation."

"Oh, I know Miss Madill helped. She told me a friend of yours I haven't met, with a French name, also helped. But regardless of that, it was your determination and love that counts most."

Mr. Boppington's happy voice came from behind Buster. "I have even more good news," he said. "Last night I received a call from the downtown office of the bank. I've been offered, and accepted, Mr. Gonifman's position. I'll be a senior vice president and the manager of my branch. There's also a very generous raise to go with the promotion," he beamed.

Buster squealed with delight. "This is going to be the happiest Thanksgiving we've ever had!"

Mr. Boppington put his hands on Buster's shoulders. "Young man, today is indeed a wonderful Thanksgiving and I have a little surprise for you."

"What kind of a surprise?" Buster asked eagerly.

Mr. Boppington smiled. "On your birthday, your mother and I felt that you weren't mature enough to play with your chemistry set. But you have proven that you are indeed responsible enough."

Mrs. Boppington hugged Buster and kissed him on the cheek. "Make sure you're careful and learn all you can from your experiments. Who knows, someday you may discover something miraculous."

Buster looked at Nappy and winked. "Miraculous, Mom? Miraculous?" Suddenly Buster Boppington could not stop laughing.